peg + cat
The Pizza Problem

JENNIFER OXLEY
+ BILLY ARONSON

**CANDLEWICK
ENTERTAINMENT**

"MAMMA MIA!" said Peg.
"It's a perfect day for pizza!"

2+1=3

Peg and Cat had just opened their restaurant for lunch. **Peg's Pizza Place** was open for cheesy, saucy business!

"Look!" gasped Cat. "Here come our first customers of the day!"

"And our coolest!" said Peg.

In walked...

Tessa, Mora, and Jesse -- the Teens!

"Hi, Teens!" said Peg.

"Hi, preteen," said the Teens.

After seating the Teens at their favorite table,
Peg and Cat took their orders.

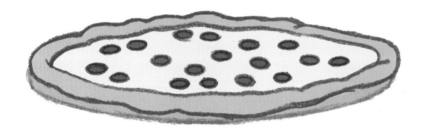

"I'll have a **whole** pizza pie," said Jesse.

"One **whole** pie for me, too," said Tessa.

"Half a pie for me," said Mora.

"WHAT-A-PIE?" asked Peg.

"Half a pie," Mora answered.

5+1=6

Peg and Cat backed into the kitchen --
and panicked!

"What in the world is **half** a pie?" asked Peg.
"Why can't Mora order a **whole** pie like every
other teenager? How can we make **half** a pie
when we don't know what a **half** is?"

Peg and Cat had a BIG PROBLEM!

Luckily, Ramone and Mac were there to explain.

"Here's a **whole** pizza,"
said Mac.

"And we're going to
cut it into two."

He pointed to one side of the pizza.
"That's a **half.**"

"And that's a **half,**" said Ramone,
pointing to the other side.

"There are two **halves** in every **whole!**"
they sang together in perfect harmony.

"I get it," said Peg.
"Each **half** pie is a
SEMICIRCLE."

8+1=9

Peg served the Teens
the two and a half pizzas, singing,
"PROBLEM SOLVED!
The problem is solved!"

9+1=10

"Want anything else?" Peg asked.

"Yeah!" said Tessa. "More singing!
To celebrate my cousin's best
friend's **half** birthday.
She's thirteen and a **half!**"

"It's not every day someone turns
thirteen and a **half,**" said Cat.
So Peg and Cat sang and danced.

Just as they were finishing
their song...

10+1=11

...more customers arrived.

"Hey, Three Bears!" said Peg and Cat.

"Hey, one Peg and one Cat," said Papa
Bear. "We're hungry for some of your
Peg-a-licious pizza."

11+1=12

Cat continued dancing to
keep the Teens entertained.

Papa Bear ordered one pizza.
Mama Bear ordered one pizza.
Baby Bear ordered one pizza.
"And another **half!**" said Baby Bear.

Peg circles and a half circle illustration.

"So that makes one, two, three
and a **half** pizzas," said Peg.

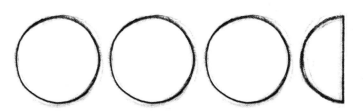

Peg served the Bears. But the Bears wanted Peg
and Cat to do a song and dance for them, too!

"Everybody wants just the right amount of pizza
while also being entertained!" said Peg.
"Keeping all our customers happy is going to be
a REALLY BIG PROBLEM!"

Peg took out her ukulele and started to sing,
"Pizza served!
The pizza is served!"

But just as she was finishing her song...

13+1=14

14+1=15

...two more customers came into **Peg's Pizza Place.**

It was
Ludwig Van Beethoven.

And
Zebra Guy!

15+1=16

"I'll take **half** a pizza," said Zebra Guy.

"And I'll take zee other **half,**" said Beethoven.

Mac chimed in. "So that's **one whole** pizza for the two of you. Because...

There are two **halves** in every **whole!**"
sang Mac and Ramone.

After serving Beethoven and Zebra Guy
and entertaining the Bears and the Teens,
Peg and Cat were exhausted.

17+1=18

"Finally, we can take a nice relaxing break," Peg said.

"WE WANT SECONDS!"

called a chorus of voices from the dining room.

"Our break just broke," said Cat.

18+1=19

The customers had eaten their pizza
and were still hungry!

The Teens wanted to share another **half** pie.

The Three Bears wanted to share another **half** pie.

Zebra Guy wanted another **half** pie.

And Beethoven wanted a **whole** pie.

In the kitchen, Mac had
some bad news for Peg.

"We only have enough ingredients to
make two and a **half** more pizzas."

"But the customers just gave us four more orders!" said Peg. "At **Peg's Pizza Place,** we ALWAYS keep the customers satisfied! I am TOTALLY FREAKING OUT!"

Cat held up his paws.

"Cat's right," said Mac.

22+1=23

"You should count backward from five to calm down."

As Peg counted, Mac and Ramone made
the last pizzas of the day.

Cat cut one of those pizzas in half
and was about to take a bite...

"That's it!" said Peg. "You amazing
half-loving Cat!"

"Huh?" asked Cat.

"Sing it!" Peg said to Mac and Ramone.

"There are two **halves**
in every **whole!**" they sang.

"Though we have four orders to fill,
some of the orders are for only half a pie,"
Peg explained. "So we might have enough
pizza for everybody! Let's count.

25+1=26

26+1=27

"The Teens ordered **half** a pie.

So did the Bears.

And Zebra Guy.
That's one and
a **half** pies.

Beethoven ordered
one **whole** pie.

27+1=28

If you add one to one and a half, that
makes a total of two and a half pies!
That's what we have!

WOOO-HOOO!"

28+1=29

"Everybody got all the pizza and entertainment they wanted!" said Peg.

"Math keeps your customers satisfied," said Cat.

"And so...

Problem solved!

The problem is solved!

We solved the problem,

so everything is awesome.

Problem solved!"

30+1=31

First edition 2016

Library of Congress Catalog Card Number 2015936917
ISBN 978-0-7636-7559-2

15 16 17 18 19 20 APS 10 9 8 7 6 5 4 3 2 1

Printed in Humen, Dongguan, China

This book was typeset in OPTITypewriter.
The illustrations were created digitally.

Candlewick Entertainment
An imprint of Candlewick Press
99 Dover Street
Somerville, Massachusetts 02144

visit us at www.candlewick.com

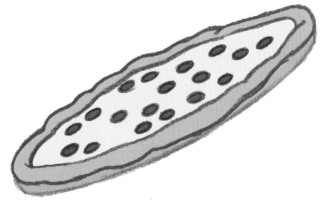